THE TIME DETECTIVES

THE MYSTERY OF
MADDIE
MUSGROVE

10

ReadZone Books Limited

50 Godfrey Avenue
Twickenham
TW2 7PF
www.ReadZoneBooks.com
© in this edition 2014 ReadZone Books Limited

This print edition published in cooperation with Fiction Express, who first published this title in weekly instalments as an interactive e-book.

Fiction Express
First Floor Office, 2 College Street,
Ludlow, Shropshire SY8 1AN
www.fictionexpress.co.uk **3 0 2015**

Find out more about Fiction Express on pages 72–73.

Design: Laura Durman & Keith Williams
Cover Image: Shutterstock Images
Printed in Spain by Edelvives

© in the text 2014 Alex Woolf
The moral right of the author has been asserted.

ISBN 978-1-783-22459-3

THE TIME DETECTIVES

THE MYSTERY OF
MADDIE
MUSGROVE

ALEX WOOLF

What do other readers think?

Here are some comments left on the Fiction Express
blog about this book:

"Maddie Musgrove just keeps getting better! :D"
Monica, Tamworth

*"Alex Woolf I love all your books especially
Maddie Musgrove!!!!!!"*
S Sara, Leeds

*"Alex your chapters are wicked and cool. I really like
them a lot because there are loads of surprises".*
Harroop, Nottingham

*"The class did enjoy 'The Mystery of Maddie
Musgrove'. In fact, they broke into spontaneous
applause at the end of it!"*
**Sue Burn and Year 5, St Matthew's C of E
Primary School, Gloucester**

"This book is so good :)"
D. Kaur Sangha, Northamptonshire

Contents

Chapter 1   An Amazing Discovery   7

Chapter 2   A Sad Story   12

Chapter 3   House of Secrets   18

Chapter 4   Gathering Evidence   27

Chapter 5   A Brush with the Law   31

Chapter 6   More Suspects   39

Chapter 7   A Disaster and a Breakthrough   44

Chapter 8   A Trip to Town   49

Chapter 9   Under Arrest   56

Chapter 10   A Race Against Time   61

About Fiction Express   72

About the Author   85

I would like to thank all the wonderful children who took the time to read this story and cast their votes on the Fiction Express website. Without your contribution, this book could not have been written. I would also like to thank Laura Durman, Paul Humphrey and Gill Humphrey at Fiction Express for their invaluable advice, support and editorial comments during the writing process.

Chapter 1

An Amazing Discovery

Joe stared up in horror. A plane was falling out of the sky, trailing clouds of black smoke. It was heading straight towards him! Terrified, he turned and began to run through the graveyard. He ran so fast he lost his balance and tumbled, scratching his bare knees and banging his head on a gravestone.

Glancing behind, he saw the dark shape of the plane closing in on him, engine screaming, fire spurting from its wings. He shut his eyes tight and waited. There was a massive roar and a ripping, smashing sound. Heat from the blast scorched his face. A horrible burning smell filled his nostrils, making him choke.

Slowly, Joe opened his eyes. The plane had crashed metres from where he lay. It must have blown up on impact because there was hardly anything left but a charred, smoking wreck. The gravestone had saved his life, shielding his body from the full force of the explosion. Only the plane's tail had survived intact. Joe's blood turned cold when he glimpsed the sign on the tail. It was a black cross – the symbol of the German Luftwaffe in the Second World War.

With a shaking hand, he reached through the long grass for the smartphone that had slipped from his grasp when he'd fallen. He prayed it wasn't broken.

The screen lit up. Thank goodness!

Nervously, he touched the "Timeshift" icon, scanned the screen and then touched "Emergency return".

* * *

The scene changed immediately. He was still lying there in the churchyard, but the wreck of the plane had disappeared. It was now a peaceful, sunny day. The only smell was fresh-mown grass, and the only sound was birdsong. Everything, in fact, was exactly as it ought to be.

A wave of relief washed through him. Had he dreamed the whole thing? It hadn't felt like a dream. And his face still felt tender from the burning heat.

"Joe! Where are you?"

He looked up to see his cousin Maya walking along the path towards the churchyard. Joe climbed gingerly to his feet.

"Hey, cuz!" she cried when she saw him. "I've been looking all over for you. What are you doing here? And what's happened to your face?"

Joe touched his sore cheek. His finger came away covered in soot. He hesitated, unsure what to say. He didn't know his cousin that well. He felt sure she'd laugh at him if he started telling her he'd just been back in time to the Battle of Britain. After all, she'd spent most of the past three days laughing at him for his strange country ways. That was when she wasn't completely ignoring him.

Joe had been sent to stay with Maya and her dad, Uncle Theo, here in Slade Common in south-east London. His parents thought it would do him good to spend some time with his relatives, instead of idling away his summer holiday reading detective stories at home in Dorset.

"It'll be fun!" his mum had assured him. "Your Uncle Theo's a historian, and you like history, don't you, Joe?"

That much was true. Uncle Theo *was* a historian, and Joe *did* like history. But what his mum hadn't told him was that Uncle Theo would be so busy writing his history books that he'd have hardly any time for Joe.

That meant Joe was forced to spend all his time with Maya.

She was Joe's age, but about as different from him as it was possible to be. Where Joe was quiet and polite, she was loud and rude. And she was *always* on the phone or texting her friends. She had about a hundred thousand of them, or so it seemed.

Joe could count his own friends on the fingers of one hand. He preferred books to people, if he was honest. And the books he loved most were detective stories. He'd read so many, he reckoned he could solve any crime. One day he'd be a famous detective. All he needed was a mystery to make his name – a mystery worthy of his talents.

As for Maya, he doubted she had time for mysteries. All she ever read were her friends' text messages.

She'd been on the phone just now in fact. She and Joe had been walking along the high street when Sarah (or was it Serena or Samantha or Susannah?) had called her. Bored with waiting for the conversation to end, Joe had wandered into the churchyard. He'd been standing by an overgrown grave when he'd spotted it, in the undergrowth at the foot of the gravestone – a smartphone. Joe had picked it up. The phone was bound to have the owner's details somewhere in it. He could return it to the owner himself – and perhaps get a reward.

So imagine his surprise when he'd switched it on and read this:

Hello Joe Smallwood.
Which time would you like to visit?

Joe had been struck dumb. How could a phone he'd just found possibly know his name? He'd never been to this place before.

At least the question had seemed innocent enough – at first. Joe had assumed it would take him to a history website.

Beneath the question were some wheels that you could spin with your fingers: one wheel for the date, one for the month and one for the year. He'd spun the wheels to 18th August 1940, expecting to be given some facts about what had happened on that date in history. Next thing he knew, a loud drone was filling his ears and a German warplane was hurtling through the sky towards him!

The phone had actually sent him back in time.

Chapter 2

A Sad Story

"Joe?" Maya asked. "You okay?" She was standing near the churchyard gate, frowning at him.

"Yeah, um, fine thanks. Just… just thought I'd look around. I fell over."

"Yeah well, whatever!" said Maya, only half concentrating. "Just don't run off again without telling me, yeah? Dad'll kill me if I lose you."

She had one eye on her phone, no doubt reading a text message.

Joe looked down again at the gravestone to see which dead person had just saved his life. The gravestone was all chipped and mossy with age. Joe could just about make out the words:

Madeleine Musgrove
Born 1st March 1827
Died 26th August 1840
By thy deeds so shall ye be judged

The girl had been 13 when she died – about the same age as Joe.

"Thanks, Madeleine Musgrove," he murmured under his breath.

"You what?" said Maya, looking up. "Did you say Madeleine Musgrove?" She looked at the gravestone. "Oh yeah, a sad story that."

"What happened to her?" asked Joe.

"Dad said Maddie Musgrove was hanged… for stealing her mistress's jewellery."

"But she was only 13!"

Maya smiled. "They used to hang children as well as adults in those days." She seemed to enjoy the look of shock on Joe's face.

"Dad researched it for the book he's writing on the history of Slade Common." She continued. "He says she was a maidservant at our house."

Theo and Maya's home was a big, crumbling old house in the oldest part of Slade Common. It was called Mycroft Place. Joe had never imagined servants working there.

"Dad thinks she was probably innocent," said Maya.

"How does he know?" Joe's skin tingled, the way it did when he thought he'd solved the mystery in one of his detective stories.

"I dunno. He thinks there were others in the house who could've done it. The father was a violent man, so Dad says, and so was his son. Then there were the other servants, or maybe one of the guests. Dad told me all about it once."

A mad idea occurred to Joe then as his fingers closed around the phone in his pocket.

"What if we could solve it?"

She frowned at him. "What *are* you talking about, cuz?"

"The mystery of Maddie Musgrove. What if we could work out who really stole the jewellery?"

Maya shrugged. "Won't help *Maddie*, will it."

Joe stared at her, his eyes sparkling. "Maybe it would," he said quietly.

"You what?"

He showed her the phone. "I found this by one of the graves." He switched it on and showed her the message:

Hello Joe Smallwood.
Which time would you like to visit?

"It was like this when I found it – with my name and everything."

Maya laughed. "This is a joke, right, cuz? A random phone you found just happened to have your name in it? No way do I believe that."

"It's true," said Joe. "But there's more, look." He pointed to the wheels. "This is some kind of time machine. See those wheels. I spun them back to 1940 – and I actually went there!"

This time Maya's laugh had a nasty, mocking edge. "Poor Joe. That bang on the head must've done something to your brain. I think I'd better get you home."

Joe seethed. "This is no joke! I nearly died just now. A German fighter plane crashed right here in this graveyard. If it hadn't been for Maddie Musgrove, I'd be…."

But he could see she didn't believe him.

"Listen to yourself, cuz," chuckled Maya. "You've been reading way too many of those mystery stories." She took his arm. "Come on, let's go."

But Joe wasn't listening. He already knew what he wanted to do. "Don't believe me if you don't want to," he told her. "I'm going back to 1840. Uncle Theo said Maddie Musgrove was innocent. Well maybe I can prove she was."

Maddie had died on the 26th August 1840. Joe spun the wheel back to 19th August, a week before. He took a deep breath, then pressed "Go".

The light dimmed and he felt heavy drops of rain on his coat. Lightning suddenly flashed above him, followed by a crack of thunder.

Maya's grip tightened on his arm. "A thunderstorm," she cried. "Let's get out of here! Quick!"

She dashed through the churchyard gate and began racing across the common. Maya hadn't even noticed what she was wearing, but Joe had: the hem of her lacy white dress blew out behind her as she ran, and her hat flew off her head. He looked down at his own clothes: a loose black tunic over an open shirt, and heavy brown trousers and boots. A chill ran through him. He'd done it! They were back in Maddie's time!

He chased after Maya through the rain, stooping briefly to pick up her hat. She reached the edge of the common and began running along the road towards Mycroft Place. Then he saw her stop and look about in disbelief. The housing estate was gone. In its place were fields. The high street was a country lane. When Joe caught up with her. Maya was shaking. She stared at him with frightened eyes. "Joe, what's happened? Where are we?" Then she noticed her dress and gasped.

"We haven't gone anywhere," said Joe gently, handing Maya her hat. "We're still in Slade Common. But now it's 1840."

He followed her as she wandered in a daze up to the entrance of Mycroft Place. Everything looked brand new. The crumbling grey brickwork was now creamy white. Even the ancient fir trees bordering the front garden looked freshly planted.

"You were right, cuz," she whispered. "I'm sorry I laughed at you."

Outside the gate was a notice:

Help Wanted:
Scullery Maid and Apprentice Footman.
Apply within.

"Look at this," said Maya, excitedly.

But before Joe could reply they were startled by a whinnying sound behind them. They whirled round to see a huge man on a black horse. He was approaching them through the gate of Mycroft Place.

The man's red face was twisted in an angry scowl. "What are you two rogues doing sniffing around here? Another pair of thieves after my wife's jewellery I'll be bound. Be off with you if you don't want to feel the sting of my whip!" Then he turned his horse and galloped off down the road.

Suddenly, Joe didn't feel quite so brave any more. "I don't like the look of him," he said. "L-let's go back to our own time. Maybe we should talk to your Dad and find out more about this place first. Perhaps he can help us solve the mystery."

"No," said Maya suddenly. "You know what Dad's like. He'll probably say we should hand your phone over to the police. Look, this is perfect, don't you see? We can apply for these jobs. That way we can get inside the house and spy on the people living there. You wanted to play detective. Well here's our chance."

"But you said the father and son were horrible," said Joe, alarmed at this sudden change in Maya. "And if *he's* anything to go by…." He went on, looking after the rider disappearing down the lane.

But Maya was determined….

Chapter 3

House of Secrets

Joe followed cautiously behind Maya as she strode confidently up the gravel driveway and knocked at the front door. It was opened by a handsome young man in a tail coat, knee breeches, stockings and buckled shoes. "Yes?" he demanded.

"We've come about the jobs," said Maya.

The man smiled unpleasantly. "Servants' entrance!" he snapped, pointing to the corner of the house where some steps led down to the basement.

"Don't you know who I am?" cried Maya, as Joe dragged her away. "He can't talk to me like that!" she spluttered. "This is my house!"

"Not yet it isn't," said Joe, leading her down the steps and around the corner of the house.

Joe knocked on the basement door. After a short wait, a tall woman with a gaunt face and high cheekbones appeared. She stared coldly at them while Joe explained their business.

"We see you're looking for...."

"I know why you're here," she said, grudgingly. "You'd better come in."

They entered a gloomy corridor of yellow walls and scuffed brown tiles. Maya stared around her in shock. "This isn't like home at all," she murmured.

A skinny girl, who was sweeping the floor, looked up and gaped at Joe and Maya.

"Lizzy," the tall woman barked at her. "Go and tell Mr Simmons that we have an applicant for apprentice footman."

"Yes, Missus." The girl skidded down the corridor and up the stairs.

"I'm Mrs Ellis, housekeeper at Mycroft Place," the woman told Joe and Maya. "You, young man, wait here. The butler will see you shortly…. Young lady, follow me."

* * *

Just half an hour later, Joe and Maya found themselves hired as servants at Mycroft Place. Maya, dressed in her rough maidservant's clothes, was sent upstairs to clean the hearth in the drawing room. Joe, decked out in his livery of blue dress-coat, striped waistcoat, black knee-length breeches and white stockings, was told to report to James, the footman, who was in the servants' hall having his lunch. Joe was about to enter when an angry-sounding whisper from within made him hesitate.

"I hate her," he heard a young woman saying. "She's always complaining about my embroidery or the way I style her hair. The other day she found this tiny stain on a sleeve of her dress and wouldn't stop going on about it."

"Calm yourself, my love," came the voice of a young man. "D'you think I've got it any better, being the master's whipping boy? At least the mistress doesn't beat you with a stick. Now that young Davenport's gone, I get the full force of his temper."

"My poor darling," said the woman. "It must be awful for you." She sighed. "Oh, when can we be gone from this horrid house? It's torture living here under this roof and never being able to talk to you, to kiss you…."

Joe blushed. He didn't fancy breaking in on *this* conversation!

Just then, Maya came bounding up to him. "Hey, cuz! What's up?"

He put a finger to his lips and gestured for her to listen.

"We're going to need money if we want to make a life together," the young man was saying.

"When can you sell the… you know?" pleaded the woman.

Joe felt Maya stiffen. "The what?" she hissed.

"Shhh!" whispered Joe.

"Be patient, my dear," the man replied. "I'll sell them soon, I promise. I'm going to Jones the Pawnbrokers tomorrow."

Suddenly, a sharp voice erupted from the far end of the corridor. "Young lady, I didn't hire you to stand around listening at doorways! There are floors to scrub, plates to scour, potatoes to peel and fowl to pluck.

Now get in here at once!" They turned to see the tall, fearsome figure of Mrs Ellis standing there, one bony arm pointing towards the kitchen.

"Coming, Missus," said Maya, and she scooted away.

Joe plucked up his courage and entered the servants' hall. To his surprise, it was empty. A moment later, a man came strolling in – the one who'd opened, and abruptly closed, the front door. Joe wondered whether it was this man's voice he'd heard through the door before Mrs Ellis interrupted.

* * *

Joe's job seemed to consist of endless trips up and down the stairs. He carried coal and wood to the fireplaces, ran errands, served refreshments and answered the door to tradesmen. His shiny buckled shoes pinched his toes and his shoulders felt tight in his dress-coat. Why had he let Maya talk him into this? He felt the weight of his smartphone, stashed in a pocket of his knee breeches and it reassured him that he could escape from here any time he wanted. Only thoughts of helping poor Maddie and the excitement of a real investigation kept him going.

At 3 o'clock in the afternoon there came a request for tea to be served in the parlour. Joe held the tray precariously with one hand as he knocked on the door.

"Come!"

He entered to find all the members of the upper household there: Lord Josiah Bullstrode (the master), his wife Lady Gwendoline (the mistress), his son Dexter, and a man and a woman who he reckoned must be their guests.

Joe hesitated at the door.

"Get a move on, boy!" chided the red-faced Lord Bullstrode – Joe remembered him as the scary man on horseback they'd seen earlier outside the house.

Shakily, Joe set down the tray and started pouring tea into the cups. He offered the first one to Lady Gwendoline.

"Serve the guests first, you imbecile!" yelled Lord Bullstrode. "Hasn't James taught you anything?"

Shaking even more, Joe offered the cup to the female guest. The teacup rattled as he handed it to her, and some of the hot tea splashed onto the lady's hand.

"Eek!" she cried.

"Elizabeth! Are you alright?" cried Lady Gwendoline.

"Clumsy oaf!" roared Lord Bullstrode, raising his cane high above his head. "I'll teach you to scald my guests!"

Joe cowered, waiting for the blow.

"Wait! Father! Stop a moment, will you?"

Josiah hesitated as Dexter Bullstrode, his equally big, curly-haired son, stepped forwards. He stared down at Joe. "Don't I know you, boy? You look familiar to me! Have you worked here before?"

"N-no, Sir," said Joe.

"It's quite alright, Josiah," said Elizabeth. "I'm fine, really."

"Leave him, my darling," said Gwendoline "You can deal with the boy later when our guests have gone."

Later that afternoon, Joe was polishing the silver in the butler's pantry when Maya popped her head in.

"Over here, cuz!" she beckoned in a loud whisper.

He got up and followed her down the corridor, through the empty kitchen, into the scullery and beyond, into a dark and tiny cell.

"This used to be Maddie's room," she told him, lighting a candle. "Now it's mine."

There was barely space for both of them in the room. In the dim, flickering light, Joe glimpsed a straw mattress and an old chest of drawers. He wrinkled his nose at the horrible smell of dirty laundry filtering through from the scullery.

"You have to pity the girl, having to spend all her days down here," said Maya sadly. "But look, I found this at the back of one of the drawers."

She showed Joe a tattily bound notebook. "Her diary!" declared Maya. Joe flicked through the pages of barely legible handwriting.

"Listen, I've been talking to Lizzy, the housemaid. She told me the jewellery was stolen on 11th July," said Maya. "Now read the entry for the day before."

Joe found a short entry for 10th July. It read:

"Goin to try and get termorow off to visit mam becors shes sick agen."

"There's no entry for 11th July," said Maya, "probably because she was off on her visit. So she couldn't have stolen the jewellery, right?"

Maya stared eagerly at Joe. He could see she'd grown attached to Maddie since taking over her job. She really wanted to believe the girl was innocent. "It was that couple we heard before, in the servants' hall," said Maya. "Talking about pawning something. *They* must have stolen the jewellery. And now they're trying to sell it so they can run away and leave poor Maddie to take the blame!"

Joe left her to get back to his work. He was excited about the diary, but also a little disappointed that Maya had found it. He'd have to get to work doing some detecting of his own. But it was just so difficult with so many jobs to do….

At nine o'clock, the servants gathered for supper in the servants' hall. Cook served up a simple but delicious meal of soup, bread, cheese and thick slices of ham. Joe's muscles were aching by this time, and he felt as if he hadn't eaten for a week. He could see Maya was suffering, too. Her hands were red from all the scrubbing and peeling she'd done. But she wore a determined look he'd not seen before – he sensed she wanted to see this thing through – for Maddie.

The mood around the table was sombre. Today, they learned, was Maddie's trial.

"Will she be sentenced today d'you suppose?" asked Lizzy.

"I should say so," said Mr Simmons, grimly buttering his bread. "These trials don't last long. She'll know her fate by now."

"Poor love," murmured Cook.

"Shed no tears for Maddie Musgrove," said Mrs Ellis. "It's only right that she pays for her crime."

"How can you be so sure she's guilty?" Maya challenged her.

Mrs Ellis looked up sharply. "Who else could it be? A missing necklace was found in her bedroom."

Joe's heart sank when he heard this. He saw the shock and disappointment in Maya's eyes. If the jewellery had been found in Maddie's room, then she probably did steal it and there was nothing they could do to help her.

"I should have dismissed her when I caught her trying the jewellery on three weeks earlier," continued Mrs Ellis. "The girl was a dreamer. Liked to imagine herself a lady. She got what she deserved!"

"Well, I reckon it were John Davenport," ventured Lizzy. "We all know how much he hated the master and mistress for all the beatings they gave him. And before he ran away, he swore to me that he'd get his own back."

"And what evidence do you have to back up this theory, Lizzy?" asked Mr Simmons.

"The day after the jewellery were stolen, I found a broken window latch in her bedroom, didn't I?" she answered. "John could've got in that way."

* * *

"We have to go back to 11th July," Maya whispered to Joe while they were clearing away the supper things. "It's the only way of finding out the truth."

He looked at her. "Face it, Maya. It was probably Maddie – they all seem convinced."

"I don't believe that and neither does Lizzy," she said firmly.

"Maya!" said Mrs Ellis, coming into the kitchen. "Stop your chatter and start washing those dishes! Shouldn't you be somewhere else young man?"

"I need him to help me bring in a new pot of water from the well," said Maya.

Mrs Ellis looked suspicious. "Alright, but I'm keeping my eye on you two!"

As soon as Joe and Maya were alone in the scullery, Joe said: "Okay, let's do this. Let's go back to 11th July. But first I need to get some sleep. I'm so tired. I'll come and get you in three hours."

Joe stumbled back to his bedroom, next door to the butler's pantry. He pulled off his tight shoes and collapsed on his bed. After setting the alarm on the smartphone, he quickly fell asleep.

Chapter 4

Gathering Evidence

It seemed only moments later that the phone started buzzing in his ear. At first he had no idea where he was. Then, with a jolt, he remembered. He got up, and tiptoed as quietly as he could to Maya's room.

"Is that you, Joe?" he heard her whisper. "Yeah. Are you ready to do this?"

"Definitely!" she said, getting up from her bed. "Let's solve this mystery once and for all."

Joe spun the dials on the phone to 11th July. "What time did Lizzy say the theft happened?" he asked.

"The police detective reckoned it was between four and five in the afternoon, so she said."

Joe spun the time dial to 3.50 pm. "Hold on tight!"

Maya clutched Joe's arm, everything went faint and cloudy for a second, and then… they were back in the same room, but now it was light.

"Did it work?" asked Maya, sounding unsure.

"I guess so," replied Joe. He peered into the kitchen – there was no one around.

"Why do we have to creep about?" asked Maya. "They all know us here now."

"Because we're back in time again, and no-one has met us yet, remember?" Joe hissed back. "Right, let's go!"

They raced out into the corridor and up the stairs. They could hear voices in one of the rooms off the entrance hall. A door began to open. Just in time, Joe and Maya darted up another flight of stairs to the first floor.

All was peaceful in Lady Gwendoline's bedroom. Beams of dusty afternoon light shone on the bed, the dressing table… and the open drawer where her jewellery could be glimpsed sparkling: bracelets, charms, rings, necklaces, earrings. Joe noticed Maya's awestruck expression at the sight of all the gold, silver and precious stones. It was quite a collection – and its theft must have been a serious matter!

A ladder was propped up against the window. Maya looked down. An underfed boy in grubby trousers with rolled-up shirtsleeves was just getting off the bottom of the ladder. He was carrying a bundle of rags in one hand and a pail of water in the other.

"I'll bet that's John Davenport, cleaning the windows," whispered Maya. Then she noticed the broken clasp on the window. "Perhaps he took the–"

"Shhh," Joe hissed as footsteps approached along the passageway. Looking around desperately for somewhere to hide, they spotted a large wardrobe. They dived inside just as someone entered the room.

Through a crack in the wardrobe door, they glimpsed Amelia, the lady's maid. She was a pale girl with pretty red curls showing under her cap. She was humming softly to herself. Was she nervous? Joe couldn't be sure. She moved to the far side of the room, towards the dressing table and its jewellery drawer. A minute or so later, she left the room. This time she had her back to them, and they couldn't tell if she'd been carrying anything.

"You see!" cried Maya, struggling out from beneath Joe. "It was either John Davenport or the lady's maid! She's probably the woman we overheard in the servants' hall!"

"But did she take the jewels?"

Before they could step out of the wardrobe and check, the bedroom door opened again.

The girl at the door looked about her, then tiptoed in. She was small and pretty with brown eyes and dark hair parted in the centre. "It's Maddie!" whispered Maya. "So she didn't go to her mum's after all."

The girl moved slowly through the room, her big eyes shining as her hand caressed the antique clock and the jewelled hairbrush on the dressing table.

This is her favourite room, thought Joe. She can dream here.

Maddie took a necklace from the drawer and held it around her neck. She began waltzing around the room, admiring herself in the large mirror on the wall.

Hearing a heavy step on the landing outside, she quickly took off the necklace and put it back where she'd found it. The door flew open and there stood Dexter Bullstrode, rather worse for drink, even though it was only the middle of the afternoon. Maddie quickly made her way back towards the door, curtsied and escaped from the room. The large man's eyes followed her as she went.

Dexter went over to a small table beneath the mirror, on which stood a decanter of wine and some glasses. He clumsily poured himself a glass, splashing some as he did so. He was about to take a swig when he heard a noise behind him. Putting down his wine, he turned, marched up to the wardrobe and flung open the doors.

"What's going on?" he cried. "Who the devil are you?"

Chapter 5

A Brush with the Law

Joe crouched there in the wardrobe, paralysed with fear, as Dexter Bullstrode fixed him and Maya with his bloodshot eyes. The big man swayed slightly, grabbing the door to steady himself. "Well?" he bellowed. "Answer me!"

At that moment, the bedroom door creaked open behind him and a woman stepped in: "Dexter, are you alright?" she asked.

Joe recognized the woman as the guest he'd spilt tea on – or rather, the one he was going to spill tea on in about five weeks' time.

"Elizabeth," muttered Dexter, turning to look at her.

The next thing Joe knew, there was a blur of movement to his left, and Maya leapt out of the wardrobe like a wildcat, sending Dexter toppling backwards. The man flailed desperately, trying to catch hold of the bedpost, but couldn't stop himself falling heavily to the floor.

"Come on, Joe!" cried Maya as she ran to the window

and quickly scrambled out onto the ladder. In a daze, Joe followed her down. From above came a roar of anger.

"Come back here, you young devils!" Dexter shook the ladder, causing Joe to lose his footing. He fell the last five rungs, landing painfully in a flower bed. His nose pressed into the mud, he found himself staring at a large boot print. With no time to think about what it might mean, he quickly followed Maya out of the flowers. They raced across a lawn and plunged head first into an overgrown area of trees and bushes.

Joe groaned, rubbing his sore arm.

"Shhh!" hissed Maya, pointing through the trees. A man was standing about ten metres away with his back to them, staring through a pair of binoculars into the trees, as if bird-watching. Joe recognized him as the Bullstrodes' other guest, the husband of Elizabeth. He and Maya crouched motionless, breathing as quietly as they could.

Eventually, the man moved further off into the bushes and disappeared from sight.

"Phew!" said Maya. "That was close!"

Joe didn't reply. He was staring at the plants around them as an idea occurred to him. He began breaking off the yellow tube-like heads of the plants and stuffing them in his pockets.

"What are you doing, cuz?" said Maya. "This is hardly the time for a nature study."

"Club moss spores," muttered Joe. "Could be useful. You'll see."

Maya shrugged and peered through the trees towards Lady Gwendoline's bedroom window.

"All clear," she said. "Let's sneak back into the house and continue investigating."

He looked up at her admiringly. She might be a loudmouth, and she might be rude sometimes, but his cousin had guts, no denying it.

"First let's check out a footprint I saw by the ladder," said Joe.

After a hurried look left and right, they dashed back across the lawn to the flower bed.

"It could be the window cleaner's," said Maya, looking down at it.

"No," said Joe, pointing out some smaller, lighter footprints. "These are the window cleaner's. He was a boy, remember. This belongs to a man. And it's fresh. He was here very recently. The question is why."

"Looks like we may have found ourselves another suspect," said Maya. "We can check out the cloakroom for any boots that match this tread."

Joe spotted a fallen slate tile by the wall, and placed it on top of the footprint to protect it.

"How do we get back in the house?" asked Joe. "They'll all be on the look-out for us by now."

Maya smiled. "The last thing people expect after a break-in is another break-in, right? Besides, I know this house. There are other ways in…." She led him round the back to a pair of wooden doors that stuck out at an angle at the base of the wall. "Like the coal chute, for example!" She pulled open the doors.

Joe stared at the soot-stained slope leading down into the dark, filthy cellar. "Do you really expect me to–"

"Come on," she said, pushing him in. Joe tumbled down the chute, landing in a heap on the cold stone floor. He coughed in the dusty air, then quickly moved aside as Maya came flying down after him.

"Right," she said, immediately getting to her feet. "Let's get back upstairs to see if the jewellery's been stolen yet. Then we can check out the cloakroom."

Joe coughed again, brushed himself down as best he could, and followed.

As they crept through the house, they heard sounds of hushed and alarmed voices. So the theft must have already happened.

From the servants' hall, Joe overheard Mr Simmons the butler saying in a shrill voice: "No one is to enter the room. Everything must be left exactly as it is until the police arrive."

Lady Gwendoline's bedroom turned out to be empty and unguarded. As Maya had said, the last thing anyone was expecting was another break-in.

The jewellery drawer was empty. "We'd better get out of here before the police arrive," said Maya.

"Wait," said Joe. He took a handful of the club moss spores from his pocket and laid them on the dressing table. He broke one open and let the fine yellow powder inside fall onto the brass handle of the jewellery drawer.

"Now what are you up to?" asked Maya impatiently.

"In one of the detective stories I read, the hero used this stuff as fingerprint powder."

Maya shook her head in wonder. "I never would've thought reading those crime books could come in so handy."

"Fingerprinting won't be invented for another fifty years," said Joe, as he peered closely at the drawer, "so we can't expect the police to find this sort of evidence.... *Voilà!*"

"What?"

"Found one!" said Joe, pointing to a pattern of tiny ridges in the powder. "Now all I have to do is find a way of lifting it."

He put his hands in his pockets and had a think. His right hand felt the outline of the smartphone.

Bingo!

He took it out and ripped off its clear, sticky protective cover. Using a small pair of scissors, which he found on the dressing table, Joe cut the plastic into strips. He laid one of these very carefully over the print, then lifted it off. The print showed clearly on the transparent plastic. He ripped a strip of blank paper from a letter pad he discovered in one of the drawers. Using a fountain pen found in the same drawer, he wrote 'drawer handle', and stuck it below the fingerprint.

Joe now moved over to the broken latch on the window to see if he could find any prints there.

"Hurry," said Maya. "The police'll be here any minute."

While waiting anxiously for him to finish, she looked more closely at the letter on top of the pad. It was signed in flowery handwriting, 'Lady Gwendoline Bullstrode'. Maya quickly scanned its contents. It was written to Gwendoline's aunt and was full of dull news about people she'd never heard of. Then she came across this paragraph at the end:

35

Dearest aunt, I fear I must now close this letter. Josiah and Dexter are at this moment engaged in another unseemly row in the next room.

They are speaking at such a volume that I fear it will attract the prying ears of the servants. Once again, Josiah is berating our son for his business failures and refusing to lend him any more money. As I do not wish the servants to know anything of Dexter's financial difficulties, I had better go and put a stop to it at once.

Yours, etc.

So, Dexter had money troubles. Interesting!

"Another fingerprint!" announced Joe triumphantly. "And it's different from the first one. So the window latch breaker and the drawer opener must have been different people."

They heard approaching voices from outside. Maya ran to the door and opened it a crack. "OMG, there are people coming up the stairs!" she gasped. "It'll be the police!" They both glanced at the wardrobe, but there was no way they'd get away with that again! They had to get out of the room, and fast. Maya poked her head out, then gestured for Joe to follow. They ran down a short passageway and up a narrow, twisting stairwell. "This leads to the attic," she said.

The attic turned out to contain several servants' bedrooms off a low-ceilinged corridor.

"That belongs to Amelia, the lady's maid," said Maya, spotting a dress hanging up in one of the rooms. "This must be her room." She began pulling open drawers. "Maybe the jewels are in here."

While Maya searched, Joe went to work dusting for prints. He quickly found one on the sewing machine.

"No sign of the jewels," sighed Maya after a lengthy search. "She must have hidden them somewhere else – if she's the thief."

"This print doesn't match either of the other two," said Joe.

"So much for your fancy forensics work," Maya scoffed. "We've now got three different prints, and we're no nearer solving the crime!"

Joe bit back his irritation. "At least we can rule out Amelia as a suspect," he said gruffly.

They waited a quarter of an hour in Amelia's room, until they heard footsteps descending the staircase below. Then they slipped out and made their way downstairs. The main parts of the house were quiet as they crept furtively to the cloakroom off the entrance hall.

Joe immediately spotted a pair of tan leather walking boots with fresh mud on them. Their treads looked identical to the boot print in the flower bed. "I'll bet you this matches," he said, suddenly anxious to prove to Maya that he was a good detective.

"Matches what, sonny?" came a smooth, silky voice behind them.

They both whirled around to see a tall man staring at them from the entrance to the cloakroom. He had a long, thin nose and grey eyes, as watchful as a hawk's, and he wore a dark blue cape.

The man came further into the room. "I am Inspector Hilliard Soames of the Yard." He gave a short bow. "I understand all the servants have been instructed to gather in the drawing room for interview, so I'm wondering why you two are here, in the cloakroom?"

"C–cleaning boots," improvised Maya.

"Inspector," boomed the voice of Josiah Bullstrode. Heavy footsteps approached. "Where are you, Inspector?"

"In here," replied Soames, without taking his eyes off Joe and Maya.

Joe pulled the smartphone from his pocket. He spun the dials, grabbed Maya's hand, took a deep breath and pressed "Go". Soames, now wearing a puzzled frown, faded into greyness.

Chapter 6

More Suspects

When they could see properly again, they found themselves still in the cloakroom – but when? Joe looked down at the phone: "20th August 1840," he read. "We're back where we began, but one day later."

"Those tan leather boots are still here though," noted Maya.

A message was blinking on the phone's screen:

Power low! Recharge! Further timeshifts dangerous!

"I'll have to recharge the phone," Joe said.

"How are we going to do that?" asked Maya. "Electricity hasn't been invented yet, remember? We might be stuck here!"

Joe felt a ripple of fear as the words "stuck here" echoed through his mind. There must be some way of recharging it. But where did people get power from before plug sockets?

"We'll have to risk one more timeshift home," said Maya. "Then we can recharge the phone and come back here and save Maddie."

"And what if the battery goes dead while we're halfway between times?" Joe pointed out. "We could be stuck in a sort of no-time limbo forever, just drifting. Do you want to risk that?"

"Sounds better than slaving away for the Bullstrodes for the rest of my life!" muttered Maya.

Joe stared at the phone, turning it over in his hands. At the back was a small plastic cover. He opened it to reveal a solar panel.

He breathed a sigh of relief. "Looks like we can power it up with sunlight, if we can just get outside."

They were halfway to the front door when they were stopped in their tracks by a shrill cry from the far end of the hall.

"Where have you two been?" exclaimed Mrs Ellis. "I've been looking for you all morning!"

Joe stammered an apology.

"Silence, boy!" shouted the housekeeper. "Go and report to James immediately. You, Maya, come with me!"

She turned on her heel and marched away. Maya sighed, "Here we go again! See ya later, cuz." And she followed Mrs Ellis upstairs.

* * *

Joe found James in the butler's pantry. The footman was in a stinking mood. "I can't believe it," he growled as he paced back and forth. "I was all set to go into town today when Lord High-and-Mighty upstairs went and postponed our trip till next Tuesday!"

"You mean Lord Bullstrode?" Joe queried.

"Nah! I'm talking about his drunken excuse for a son."

"What's so important that it can't wait a few days?"

The footman looked up angrily. "It's just some… some urgent business, alright? None of your concern!" He bashed his hand against a wooden cabinet, making the crockery chatter.

I'll bet it was you talking about going to the pawnbrokers, thought Joe. *That's what your urgent business is!*

Just then, the parlour bell rang.

James cursed. "See what they want, will you, Joe? But first wipe that soot off your face. Where've you been all morning anyway? Down a mine?"

Luckily, James didn't seem that interested in getting an answer to his question, and Joe quickly left and went upstairs to the parlour.

Before entering, he put his ear to the door, worried in case Inspector Soames was there.

Joe recognized the voices of Dexter and another man – that guest, the bird-watching husband of Elizabeth.

"I say, Dexter, old chap," the guest was saying, "I've heard you've still got money troubles. Why not come up to town with me tonight? I know a first-class gaming house in Mayfair. You could easily double or treble your money in one evening."

"Or lose everything!" Dexter grunted in reply. "No thanks, Ambrose. I think I'll stick around here for now. There are a couple of servants we've just hired, a boy and a girl. I'm sure I've seen them somewhere before.

Anyway, I think they might be up to something and I want keep an eye on them."

Joe swallowed. He daren't go in now! Then he heard Dexter's heavy tread coming towards the door.

"Why can't anyone answer a bell around here?" Dexter thundered.

Close to panic, Joe dashed to the far end of the hallway and hid himself behind a grandfather clock.

Dexter lurched out of the room. "James!" he bawled.

At that moment there was a loud knock at the front door.

James came flying up the basement stairs. "Yes sir?"

"First answer the door," ordered Dexter. "Then come and see me."

"Yes sir."

Joe watched as James opened the door. His neck hairs prickled in alarm when he saw who the visitor was.

Inspector Soames!

James took the policeman's cape, hat and stick, then showed him into the parlour. Joe took the opportunity to flee back downstairs. He found Maya in the servants' hall. "Soames is here," he told her.

"Oh, help!" said Maya.

James poked his head in. "Oi, you two. Tea and pastries for four needed in the parlour. Cook's preparing it now. Be ready to take it up in ten minutes."

Joe and Maya stared at each other. What now?

"We have to timeshift out of here," said Maya. "Whatever the risks, it's better than being caught."

"We might not get caught," said Joe. "Soames saw

42

us for less than a minute nearly six weeks ago. We were covered in soot and in different clothes. He might not recognize us. And we disappeared before his eyes – he's not going to confess to that now, is he? If we just act normal and serve them tea and pastries, we'll be fine, and we'll be able to lift prints from the cups. See if we can find a match."

"Or we could just run," said Maya softly.

"Maybe," said Joe. "If we hide out in the garden, we can recharge the phone. I'm really worried about that battery running out and leaving us stranded." He sighed. "But to reach the garden, we'd have to get past James, Simmons and Mrs Ellis. One of them's bound to spot us before we make it out of here."

"Well, be quick and decide," said Maya, urgently.

Chapter 7

A Disaster and a Breakthrough

Maya stared at the phone in Joe's hand. He could see she really wanted him to use it, but the flashing message on the screen – *Further timeshifts dangerous!* – scared him. He just couldn't bring himself to risk it.

They were alone in the servants' hall. Any second now, Cook would summon them to take the tea things up to the parlour.

"We have to get out of here!" urged Maya. "If you won't use the phone, we'll have to make a run for it and hope for the best."

"We'll never get past Ellis," said Joe. "I swear that woman's got eyes in the back of her head."

"There's always a chance," Maya coaxed. "We'll be sitting ducks if we stay here and serve tea to Soames and Dexter. One of them's bound to recognize us."

"Okay" shrugged Joe. He went to the door and peeped out into the basement corridor. There were sounds of bustling activity from the kitchen, but for now the corridor was empty.

The two of them tiptoed silently out of the servants' hall, then quickly bolted up the stairs.

They sprinted down another empty corridor. So far, their luck was holding. But as Joe emerged into the entrance hall, he caught sight of Simmons the butler. Joe ducked back into the corridor, hushing Maya with a finger to his lips. From the shadows, he watched Simmons enter the drawing room opposite. Joe made a dash for the the front door.

"What in heaven's name are you doing, boy?" demanded Mrs Ellis, trapping him in the prison of her steel-grey stare. She approached him menacingly from the staircase. "Come with me this instant!"

Joe bowed his head in defeat and began following her back along the corridor.

To his surprise, Maya had disappeared. Then he glimpsed the top of her mop cap peeping out from behind the leaves of a large pot plant. Bending briefly, he slid the phone along the smooth tiles towards her hiding place – at least if Maya escaped, she'd be able to recharge it. Then he hurried after Mrs Ellis.

"Where's Maya?" snapped Mrs Ellis when they'd reached the kitchen.

"I–I think Lizzie needed her help with something," stammered Joe. "One of the guests wanted some hot water carrying up – f–for a bath."

Mrs Ellis seemed to have only two expressions: angry or suspicious. Right now, she was wearing both of them.

"I'm sure Joe can manage the tea by hisself," interrupted Cook with a kindly smile. Joe eyed the two sturdy trays filled to the brim with tea and pastries. He would have to make two trips.

In the parlour, he found Soames, Lord and Lady Bullstrode, Dexter and the two guests, who he now knew as Ambrose and Elizabeth. When Joe entered, Soames started from his seat, his face turning pale, but he said nothing.

"Something the matter with you, Inspector?" harumphed Lord Bullstrode.

"Er… no, nothing. Nothing at all." Soames shook his head as if to clear it of an irrational thought. "As I was saying, sir, you'll be pleased to hear that the trial proceeded very smoothly. Very smoothly indeed. Despite Miss Musgrove's pleas of innocence, her guilt was plain for everyone in the courtroom to see."

Joe felt Dexter's bloodshot eyes on him as he began pouring the tea. Dexter had also noticed Soames' jump of surprise when Joe had walked in.

"Is there any news regarding the whereabouts of the rest of my jewellery?" enquired Lady Bullstrode.

"I fear not, your Ladyship," replied Soames.

"I wonder what that wretched girl did with it."

"On that we can only speculate." said Ambrose.

* * *

An hour later, Joe was summoned to clear away the dirty tea things. Instead of taking them directly to the kitchen, he first went to his bedroom, removed the sticky plastic phone cover from its hiding place in a

46

drawer and got to work dusting the crockery for prints. While upstairs, he'd mentally noted which cups and saucers had been whose, and the first ones he tried were Dexter's. Unfortunately, Dexter hadn't left a clear print anywhere.

Lord and Lady Bullstrode did leave prints, but they didn't match either of the prints he'd lifted from Lady Bullstrode's room – Joe had been worried that the jewellery drawer print had been Lady Bullstrode's, but it wasn't, proving that it belonged to the thief.

Ambrose had been bird-watching at the time, so, unsurprisingly, his prints didn't match. But when Joe checked Elizabeth's saucer, he got a surprise. Here he found a thumb print identical to the one he'd found on the broken window latch. His first match! So Elizabeth was involved somehow. But why would she break the window latch? Maybe to allow an accomplice to enter the room? She seemed such a stylish, elegant lady – hardly the type to…. But then wasn't it odd how quickly she'd arrived on the scene on the day of the theft. As soon as Dexter discovered him and Maya in the wardrobe, Elizabeth had come into the room – almost as if she'd been waiting outside.

* * *

Joe couldn't wait to tell Maya this news, but their paths didn't cross again until supper. Then it was impossible to talk under the eagle-eyed glare of Mrs Ellis. Maya looked exhausted. She toyed with her food in sullen silence, not meeting anyone's eyes. When the two of them finally found themselves alone in the scullery, Joe asked her what was wrong.

"You should have let us timeshift out of here, Joe!" she said bitterly. "After you were taken away by Ellis, I went and hid out in the stables, but got spotted by the groom, and he physically dragged me back to the house. Ellis went mad and whacked me with her carpet beater. She hasn't let me out of her sight since. I've been on my knees all day, scrubbing floors, sweeping ashes, cleaning grates. Look at my hands! Covered in blisters! And all because you were too chicken to use your phone!"

"But *you* had the timephone," said Joe. "You could've used it any time."

Maya frowned at him. "You what?"

"The timephone!" said Joe desperately. "I slid it towards you when you were hiding behind that plant! I thought you could take it out into the sunlight and…." He trailed off. "Oh no! Don't tell me…."

He dashed out of the scullery.

The entrance hall, when he got there, was dark and silent. He squinted at the tiles near the pot plant, but the phone wasn't there – someone had taken it, maybe thrown it away. Then the awful truth hit him like a punch in the stomach: he and Maya were trapped in 1840!

Chapter 8

A Trip to Town

The next few days were among the grimmest of Joe's life. James kept him busy from morning 'til night. He didn't mind the physical labour as much as answering the parlour bells. On each visit, Dexter would fix him with that tipsy, distrustful stare, as if trying to remember where the devil he'd seen him before.

To make matters worse, Maya was refusing to speak to him – she blamed him for the timephone disaster. He could see she was getting more and more tense and angry with each passing day, and he knew that sooner or later she'd try and escape again, whatever the risks. Ellis could beat her as much as she liked, there was just no way a girl like Maya could accept life as a Victorian servant.

When he wasn't worrying about himself and Maya, Joe's thoughts were with poor Maddie. At least he and Maya still had their lives, but Maddie's date with the hangman was looming, and there seemed to be nothing he could do about it.

* * *

"Joe? Are you awake?" He started up from his pillow and peered into the gloom.

"Maya?" She came in and sat at the foot of his bed. "So, you're talking to me again?" he said.

"I still haven't forgiven you for losing the timephone," she replied stiffly. "And I've no idea how we're ever going to get back to our own time. But right now I'm thinking about Maddie."

"Me, too," he said.

"If we don't at least try and save her, then this whole thing's been pointless."

"I agree," said Joe, stifling a yawn. "But there's no way they'll let her go unless we can find the real thief."

"I know that, which is why I've been trying to narrow down our list of suspects. John Davenport couldn't have done it for a start."

Joe rubbed his eyes, trying to wake himself up. "How come?"

"Cook told me that he left back in June, weeks before the theft. Said he got a job 'over Sydenham way'."

Joe nodded thoughtfully. "Well, that leaves us with Dexter, James and Elizabeth – and the owner of that bootprint."

"Elizabeth?"

Joe explained about the thumbprint on the window latch.

"Good work, cuz!" Joe was pleased to see her smiling at him again.

"Tomorrow is the 25th," said Maya. "Dexter and James are going into town, remember? Joe, you simply have to go with them, so you can spy on James – see if it's the jewels he's taking to the pawnbrokers."

* * *

The next morning, before giving Joe his list of jobs, James informed him that he would be going into Bromley for the day with 'Master Dexter'.

"Can I – I mean, do you think my presence might be helpful as well?"

James shook his head. "Your place is here, boy. You leave the trips into town to your elders and betters!"

Joe's heart sank – thwarted once again. James would pawn the stolen jewels, and tomorrow morning, innocent Maddie would be hanged!

In a despairing mood, he began on his morning chores, trimming the wicks in the entrance hall oil lamps. Outside, on the forecourt, he could hear the groom preparing the gig for the trip into town. Dexter descended from his room in his frock coat, cravat and top hat. James trailed behind him in his smartest livery, carrying a package under his arm – the jewels? As they passed by, Dexter caught sight of Joe and turned to James: "I don't trust that boy. I want him with us where I can keep my eye on him."

James grimaced. He beckoned Joe with an angry jerk of his head. Elated, Joe wiped his hands on a cloth and hurried to join them.

* * *

For a twenty-first-century boy, the journey was slow and uncomfortable, especially when most of it was spent in the shadow of Dexter's watchful, unsteady gaze. The road was bumpy and full of ruts and Joe kept worrying that a wheel on the gig was about to come off. But it didn't, and they finally arrived in Bromley. The bustling high street was full of horses and carriages. Joe wrinkled his nose at the unpleasant smell of manure, coal smoke and rotting food.

Dexter ordered the driver to park the gig outside an inn. "Shan't be long," he muttered as he heaved his bulk out into the street.

Joe spotted a smile flickering at the corners of James's mouth. "Stay here and keep our driver company, will you Joe," he said as he extracted his parcel from under the seat. "He'll be in there for ages, and I have a little business to attend to."

With that, the footman got out of the gig and strode quickly up the high street.

"I also have a little business to attend to," Joe muttered to the driver, and before the man could object, he clambered out and trotted after James.

Keeping his distance, Joe followed the footman for a hundred metres or so. At one stage he lost him in the crowds of shoppers, but then, suddenly, he caught sight of him, entering a small shop with dark windows and three gold-coloured balls hanging outside the entrance: Jones the Pawnbrokers! So he was right. It *had* been James that day promising his girlfriend that he'd visit the pawnbrokers. Crouching in the doorway of a neighbouring shop, Joe waited until the footman emerged a quarter of an hour later, this time without the package.

Joe shook with excitement – the stolen jewels were right there, in that shop! James's name would be in the pawnbroker's records: proof that Maddie was innocent. Now all he had to do was go to the police and tell them about it. Joe was about to race back to the gig when he was stopped in his tracks by a shocking sight: Dexter, a heavy bag in his fist, came striding down the street towards him. To his amazement, Dexter then entered the same pawnbrokers. Puzzled and wracked with nerves, Joe had to wait a further twenty minutes before Dexter reappeared, counting a large wad of banknotes. As he swaggered along the high street, clearly the worse for drink, something fluttered from his pocket into the gutter. Joe ran over and picked it up. He had to read it several times to be sure of what he was seeing: a receipt for £500 for 'jewels'!

* * *

Back at Mycroft Place, Joe was immediately set to work preparing afternoon tea. What with that, and then family dinner, and then servants' supper, it wasn't until half past nine that he finally managed to find a quiet moment to tell Maya what he'd discovered. They were in the scullery, doing the washing up. When he told her, she nearly dropped the plate she was drying.

"Dexter!" she gasped. "That's incredible!"

"And I've got a signed receipt – so we have proof!" exclaimed Joe, triumphantly

"Clever you! And that's not all, cuz. While you were out, I also made a discovery."

"The phone!" said Joe eagerly.

Her face fell. "No. Sorry, Joe. Not that. But I'm sure it'll turn up…. No, I managed to find out who planted that bootprint."

"Who was it?"

She gave him a teasing smile. "I saw him coming back from a walk earlier today and he was wearing those same tan leather boots."

"For goodness' sake, tell me who, or I'll stab you with this fork!"

"Ambrose," she giggled.

"Ambrose?"

"Yeah. Later on, I managed to steal one of his boots and took it back to that print – y'know, just to be sure. It was still there after six weeks, protected by that slate you put on top of it. It made a perfect match, Joe!"

Joe absently rinsed a glass, deep in thought. "But Ambrose was bird-watching in those bushes that day."

"Was he?" queried Maya. "That's what we assumed, but now I reckon he must have been part of the plot. He was probably waiting under that window for Elizabeth, or maybe Dexter, to throw him the jewels. Then when he heard Dexter shouting at us, he knew something had gone wrong, and he scarpered. He was probably using those binoculars to keep watch on the window."

Just then they heard a crack of thunder, and a flash of blue lightning filled the room.

Joe peered out as rain began to spatter the window. "Maddie's due to be hanged tomorrow and we're stuck here," he said. "We've just got to tell someone what we know and save her life."

"Look," said Maya, firmly. "How about we go to the police now? Tell Soames everything. If we set off right away, we'll be there well before dawn."

"What, you mean walk all the way to Bromley in this weather?" said Joe.

"We have to do something," said Maya.

"We could go to Lady Bullstrode and tell *her* the truth. She seems the only decent person in this whole house."

Maya sneered at this. "Do you really think she'd believe us over her son?"

"She might. She'd do anything to get her jewels back." But he could see Maya wasn't convinced.

Another crack of thunder shook the house. The rain rattled and hissed against the window like an angry snake.

"I don't see that we have much choice," groaned Joe.

Chapter 9

Under Arrest

Joe and Maya crept cautiously upstairs. Low voices could be heard from the parlour. The men usually retired there after dinner for a smoke and a chat. From the drawing room, next door, came the tinkling of the piano. That was a stroke of luck! Lady Bullstrode often played the piano in there when she was alone – and right now they needed her to be alone!

Hesitantly, Joe pushed open the drawing room door, and they entered. Lady Bullstrode stopped playing and looked up, surprised.

"Yes?" she demanded.

"Mistress!" said Maya urgently. "We're here about Maddie Musgrove. We think there's been a terrible mistake."

"What do you mean, girl?"

"She never stole the jewellery," said Joe. "It was your son. It was Dexter."

Lady Bullstrode rose slowly from the piano stool and moved over to where Joe was standing. Then, to his surprise and shock, she suddenly cuffed him hard, across the head, sending him reeling.

"How dare you accuse my son of theft, you impudent little… little wretch!" she screamed.

"But it's true, your Ladyship. We've got the eviden–"

Before they could say any more, loud footsteps sounded in the hallway and Dexter burst into the room, followed by Inspector Soames and another policeman.

"Ah, there they are!" Dexter cried. "The very pair I've just been telling you about, Inspector!" He turned to Lady Bullstrode.

"Mother, I suddenly remembered earlier this evening where I'd seen these two servants of ours. They were hiding in your wardrobe on the day of the theft – no doubt part of the plot! I summoned the inspector here so that he could arrest them."

"No!" cried Maya. "It's him!" She pointed at Dexter. "He's the thief, and we've got proof! Show them, Joe. Show them the receipt!"

"What's all this?" demanded Soames.

Joe took the pawnbroker's receipt out of his pocket and passed it to Soames. The detective fished a pair of eyeglasses from his pocket and peered at it.

"I watched Mr Dexter go into a pawnbroker's yesterday, in Bromley High Street," explained Joe. "When he came out, he accidentally dropped this."

"And we've found evidence about the two guests, Ambrose and Elizabeth," added Maya. "They were also part of the plot."

"What's he given you, Inspector?" thundered Dexter. "I demand to know!"

Soames had gone quite still. He held out the receipt to Dexter and said: "Would you care to explain this, Mr Bullstrode?"

Dexter snatched it. When he saw what it was, his face went purple and his eyes nearly popped out of his head.

"Perhaps you could tell me, sir," said Soames coldly, "why you found it necessary to pawn five hundred pounds worth of jewellery less than two months after your mother's valuables went missing."

Dexter stared at Soames, then suddenly burst out laughing. "You see what they're doing here, don't you? The Musgrove girl is due to be executed tomorrow, and this pair are so desperate to save their friend's skin, they're trying to pin the crime on me! Anyone can forge a signature, Inspector. I'm surprised you of all people failed to see through their little scheme."

He crumpled the receipt in his fist and tossed it onto the fire.

Joe and Maya stared in horror as the flames licked at the small piece of paper, quickly reducing it to ashes.

"I have to say, sir," remarked Soames. "That looked genuine."

"You would do well to remember the influence the Bullstrodes have in this community, Inspector," said Lady Bullstrode. There was a menacing edge to her voice. "We can make careers, and we can also *break* them."

Soames nodded. "I understand what you're saying, your Ladyship."

Then he turned to the other police officer and gestured towards Joe and Maya. "Take these two to the cells, please, constable."

"I can't take them back to Bromley now, sir," said the policeman. "Not on a night like this."

"Alright then, take them out and lock them in the stables. And make sure you stay awake to keep an eye on them."

"Yes sir."

"He's lying!" cried Maya, and she began to struggle, but she was no match for the burly constable, who soon had her and Joe in heavy iron handcuffs.

* * *

A short while later, Joe and Maya found themselves locked up in the cold, dark stable, with its strong odour of straw and manure. In the shadows around them, horses softly snorted and whinnied in their sleep.

"What are we going to do now?" groaned Maya, leaning back against a hay bale.

Joe rubbed his sore wrists and tried to think. Whichever way he looked at it, their position seemed hopeless.

"Why did we ever do this, cuz? What were we thinking?" Maya gave a dry chuckle. "It seemed like such a brilliant idea, didn't it? Let's play time travellers! Let's save Maddie Musgrove.... And now here we are, set to join her on the gallows." She sighed. "Soon there'll be two more gravestones in that churchyard next to Maddie's.

And Dad'll wonder whatever became of us."

Maya put her face in her hands and her shoulders shook with quiet sobs. Joe just felt numb – he couldn't believe things had got this bad.

Chapter 10

A Race Against Time

Joe was woken, hours later, by the sound of the stable door creaking open and a beam of bright sunlight in his eyes. His skin prickled and itched from a night spent lying on straw. Squinting into the light, Joe saw Inspector Soames cautiously enter the stables. The inspector was looking fretful.

"Are you two alright?" he said. "I do hope your night wasn't too uncomfortable. I had to place you in custody, you see, to make Mr Bullstrode believe he'd persuaded me of your guilt and his innocence. But of course he hadn't. I knew as soon as I laid eyes on it that the receipt was genuine. And now we have to go up to town and pay a visit to Jones the Pawnbroker, who I'm sure will have kept a copy of it. We must go now, with all speed, in case Mr Bullstrode catches wind of what we're up to. You can rest assured, he will stop at nothing to destroy any copy of that receipt before we can lay our hands on it."

Hearing all this, Joe felt a surge of joy. "Thank you, Inspector!" he cried. "Thank you for believing in us."

* * *

The constable was waiting for them outside the stables with a police gig at the ready, and soon they were racing along the path that led to the main road. As they reached the gate, Joe glanced back at the house. He was shocked to see a furious-looking Dexter gaping at them from an upstairs window.

"He's seen us!" yelled Joe.

"Then he's bound to give chase," said Soames. "Fast as you can now, constable!"

The constable cracked the whip, and the gig flew out of the gate and onto the open road.

They hadn't been going more than five minutes when a black dot appeared on the road behind them. The dot quickly grew bigger, until it became recognizable as a man on horseback.

"It's Dexter," cried Maya. "He's gaining on us!"

"Faster, constable!" urged Soames.

"We're at top speed, sir!"

They entered a wood, and the road began a series of twists and turns. The gig lurched, and its passengers were flung painfully from side to side.

Dexter was close enough now for Joe to see the triumphant grin on his huge red face. The big man whipped his horse faster and was soon alongside the gig. They could hear him cackle with delight as he began to move in front. Suddenly, the constable pulled sharply on the reins as a deep puddle came in sight, a remnant of last night's storm. Dexter didn't see it, being too intent on overtaking the gig. His horse slipped in the wet mud and Dexter was thrown headfirst into a ditch. The last Joe saw of him, as they raced away, was a screaming, purple-faced figure shaking his fist at them.

* * *

Ten minutes later, they were in Bromley. Jones the Pawnbroker turned out to be very obliging. He handed Soames a copy of Dexter's receipt and also one from a certain Mr Ambrose Farnham, who had visited a few weeks earlier. Both men had deposited valuable jewels and Soames quickly verified that these matched the description of the stolen ones.

"Good work, both of you," Soames congratulated Joe and Maya as they returned to the gig.

"Now we must move, and stop the hanging!" exclaimed Maya.

Soames consulted his pocket watch. "I fear we may already be too late. It's almost ten o'clock, and she's due to hang at noon. Newgate Prison is eleven miles away. We'll never make it in time."

"We have to try!" insisted Maya.

The constable remained in Bromley, and Soames himself took the driver's seat. They reached the Old Kent Road by 11 o'clock, and Southwark by 11.20. Here, the going became slower along the cobbled streets filled with people, horses and carriages heading into or out of the city.

"Police! Emergency!" yelled Soames. "Out of my way!"

He rang a bell suspended over the driver's seat, but few of the vehicles in front paid much attention.

"Oh, for a police siren," moaned Maya.

They crossed the Thames at the Queen Street Bridge at 11.30. Ten minutes later, they were stalled in traffic on Cannon Street, still half a mile from Newgate Prison.

"I think we must accept that we've done our best," sighed Soames.

Maya reached forward and desperately rang the bell. "Get outta here!" she roared at the carriage in front. "A girl's about to die because of you!"

The driver yelled something abusive back.

"Perhaps we can make it on foot from here," Joe suggested.

Soames glanced at him, then nodded. He guided the horses to the side of the road, and the three of them jumped onto the pavement.

On Newgate Street, the crowds became thicker. Labourers, servants and factory workers filled the air with their chatter and raucous laughter. Joe sensed a gathering excitement as they drew closer to the prison on the corner of Old Bailey. Smells of unwashed bodies, roasting food and open sewers wafted in on the warm breeze, making him giddy and sick.

Two minutes to twelve.

Above them, a bell begin to toll.

"Quick!" urged Soames. "That's St Sepulchre's church. It means the execution is about to take place."

The forbidding grey walls and barred windows of the prison came into view. In front of the gate was a large black platform, about two metres high. On the platform stood two upright posts supporting a cross beam, and from the crossbeam hung a noose.

"Oh my God!" cried Maya. "There's Maddie!"

A thin, frail girl was standing near the noose, her arms tied behind her back. There were three men on the platform with her. One of them, a thickset man with a white beard, placed the noose around her neck.

The sight of this made Joe almost gag.

"Stop!" he heard Maya cry out, but her voice was drowned by the enormous cheers from the crowd.

"That's the executioner," Soames yelled. "We have to get the attention of the other fellow there, the Under Sheriff. He's the only one with the authority to stop the execution."

They tried to force their way through the dense pack of bodies.

Joe saw one of the men, a priest, step closer to Maddie and begin chanting in time with each chime of the bells. Maddie looked frozen with fear.

Suddenly, Joe couldn't see Maya. She'd been right in front of him. Now she was gone. Seconds later, he saw her re-emerge near the front of the crowd. All that lay between her and the gallows was a line of uniformed guards wielding pikes. Joe saw her pleading with one of the guards, but he was taking no notice.

Determined to get closer himself, Joe dropped to his knees and began crawling through the forest of legs. People swore and spat at him and stamped on his fingers and knuckles, but he kept going.

When he reached Maya, he found her staring, terrified, at the scene on the platform. He looked up to see that a white hood had been placed over Maddie's head.

"You've got to stop this!" Maya screamed at a guard. "She's innocent! We have evidence! Let me speak to the Under Sheriff."

"Back, you!" bellowed the guard. He didn't look as if he'd even heard her. Above them, the executioner moved his hand towards the lever, ready to open the trapdoor below Maddie's feet.

Maya's cries had caught the attention of a thin, sad-faced boy standing to her right. He had tear tracks running down his grimy face as he looked up at Maya. "Evidence?" he said earnestly. "You got… evidence?"

The executioner's hand was now on the lever.

Suddenly, before Joe even realized what was happening, the boy darted between the guard's legs and scrambled up some steps onto the platform.

He pulled at the Under Sheriff's coat. Shocked and angry, the man tried to swat him away. The executioner's hand started to pull on the lever as guards surged up onto the platform to arrest the boy.

"They got evidence!" the boy howled as he tried to fight them off.

The guards were dragging the boy away when they were stopped by another shout. Soames stormed through the gap they had left in their ranks and mounted the platform. He was waving a piece of paper that Joe recognized as the pawnbroker's receipt. The Under Sheriff stared at the receipt as Soames rapidly explained the situation. Then the Under Sheriff gestured to the executioner to stand aside.

Taking advantage of the general confusion, Joe and Maya ran up the steps. They approached Maddie, and Joe pulled the bag from her head while Maya removed the noose from her neck.

The girl blinked and looked around her. "What's 'appening?" she said in a dazed voice.

Maya hugged her. "You're free," she sobbed. "They're not – they're not going to hang you, Maddie."

When she heard this, the colour drained from Maddie's face, and she collapsed. The boy caught her in his arms. Maddie opened her eyes and gazed up at him. "John Davenport!" she murmured faintly. "Was this your doin'?"

"Not me, Maddie," he said shyly. "It were these two what stopped it."

She looked at Joe and Maya. "Who are you?"

"Your new friends," smiled Joe.

* * *

Events moved swiftly after that. An application was made to the judge for a stay of execution. The new evidence was presented and, within hours, all charges were dropped. Maddie was free to leave prison. At the same time, the judge issued warrants for the arrest of Mr Dexter Bullstrode and Mr and Mrs Ambrose Farnham.

Joe and Maya remained in the city for the afternoon, and they were there outside the prison gates at five o'clock when Maddie emerged with a small bag of her belongings. Inspector Soames, another policeman and John Davenport were also there to greet her.

As she came out, Maddie looked around her, dark eyes bright with wonder, as if she still couldn't believe she was alive. Joe was reminded of that day he'd seen her dancing around Lady Bullstrode's room, pretending to wear that necklace. The girl was a dreamer alright – and this was a dream come true.

"Am I really free?" she asked.

"You most certainly are," said Soames. "Sergeant Lovett here has just returned from Mycroft Place, haven't you, Sergeant?"

"Indeed I have sir," said the policeman. "And I can inform you that when I issued the arrests to the accused, Mrs Elizabeth Farnham immediately broke down and confessed to everything. Said it was a plot hatched by Mr Bullstrode, herself and her husband. It seems that Mr Bullstrode was in trouble from his business failures, and Mr Farnham was heavily in debt from his gambling. Mrs Farnham said she placed the necklace in your bedroom, Maddie, to try and frame you. And, in case we didn't find the necklace, she also broke the window latch in her Ladyship's bedroom to fool us into thinking it was a case of breaking and entering."

Soames placed his hands on Joe and Maya's shoulders "And if it wasn't for these two brave young people, none of this would have come to light."

When Maddie heard this, she was overcome with emotion and began to cry. "Thank you, kind strangers," she wept. "I 'ope I m-might find some means of repaying you one day."

"Just live, Maddie," said Joe, thinking of that sad little gravestone that had started this whole adventure. "Live a long and happy life."

"Do you have anywhere to stay, my girl?" Soames asked Maddie. "A relative perhaps who can offer you a bed until you find yourself another position?"

Maddie shook her head sadly.

"Well then it may have to be the workhouse for you, I'm afraid – at least temporarily."

"I may be able to 'elp there, sir," said John Davenport, stepping forward. "See, I'm a 'prentice blacksmith workin' in Sydenham, and it just so 'appens, the smith's wife is lookin' for a housemaid…."

Maddie looked up. "Really, John? D'you think she'd want me? After all what's 'appened?"

"I'll put in a good word for you," offered Soames. "Here, let me write something for you now." He took out a pad of official police notepaper, then patted his coat pockets for a pen. His hand must have touched something unexpected, because he frowned, then dug deeper into one of his pockets.

"Ah yes, I almost forgot about this," said Soames, pulling out a small, black, rectangular object.

Joe's eyes widened.

"Our phone!" cried Maya gleefully.

"Yes, I thought it belonged to you two," added Soames with a quiet smile. "I spotted it under the grandfather clock in the entrance hall at Mycroft Place while I was there yesterday evening. I suppose someone must have kicked it under there accidentally."

He handed it to Joe, who examined it carefully and was relieved to see it was undamaged. It felt warm to the touch, and he noticed it was already recharging itself in the sunlight.

Soames asked Maya and Joe if they wanted a ride back to Mycroft Place to collect any belongings.

They looked at each other, and Joe suddenly thought of exactly the place they ought to go.

"Could you just take us to the churchyard at Slade Common?" he asked.

"Of course," replied Soames.

Before getting back into the gig, they said goodbye to Maddie.

"Must you go?" cried the girl.

"I'm afraid so," said Maya. "We came here to stop a terrible injustice, and we've done that now, so there's no more reason for us to stay. Like Joe said, all we ever wanted was for you to be able to live your life. So go and live it, Maddie. And remember us, just like we'll remember you."

"I will," cried Maddie. "I promise I will."

* * *

It was getting on for evening by the time the police gig pulled up at the little church in Slade Common.

"Thanks for everything, Inspector," said Joe, as he and Maya got down.

"Not at all, young man. It's *me* who should be

thanking *you*. Good luck, whatever you do now."

Joe and Maya went through the lychgate and into the churchyard. There were fewer graves than they remembered, and the empty stretch of lawn was dappled with gold in the last rays of the sun. They wandered over to the spot where they reckoned Maddie's gravestone would one day lie. Joe took the timephone, now fully recharged, out of his pocket. He felt Maya's hand clasp his. "Take us home, cuz," she whispered.

He spun the dials and pressed 'Go'.

* * *

Gravestones suddenly appeared, like a stone forest around them. Maddie's grave was there, just as they remembered it. They walked around it to see the inscription on the other side. It read:

Madeleine Davenport
Devoted wife, mother and grandmother
Born 1st March 1827
Died 26th August 1900
May she rest in peace

THE END

FICTI●N EXPRESS

THE READERS TAKE CONTROL!

Have you ever wanted to change the course of a plot, change a character's destiny, tell an author what to write next?

Well, now you can!

'The Mystery of Maddie Musgrove' was originally written for the award-winning interactive e-book website Fiction Express.

Fiction Express e-books are published in gripping weekly episodes. At the end of each episode, readers are given voting options to decide where the plot goes next. They vote online and the winning vote is then conveyed to the author who writes the next episode, in real time, according to the readers' most popular choice.

www.fictionexpress.co.uk

WINNER
Education Resources
Award for Innovation

FICTION EXPRESS

TALK TO THE AUTHORS

The Fiction Express website features a blog where readers can interact with the authors while they are writing. An exciting and unique opportunity!

FANTASTIC TEACHER RESOURCES

Each weekly Fiction Express episode comes with a PDF of teacher resources packed with ideas to extend the text.

"The teaching resources are fab and easily fill a whole week of literacy lessons!"
Rachel Humphries, teacher at Westacre Middle School

**Have you read the second Time Detectives book
– *The Disappearance of Danny Doyle* – yet? Here
is a taster for you…**

Chapter 1

The Missing Twin

"Come on, cuz! Let's go in."

Without waiting for Joe to answer, Maya pushed open the door and entered the old, tumbledown house. The hallway was dim, the air stuffy and filled with tiny specks of dust that sparkled as they floated through the sunlight streaming in from behind her. A rickety-looking staircase curved upwards into shadow.

"We should leave," said Joe, still loitering at the doorway. "There might be someone living here."

"No way!" said Maya. "Who would live in an old dump like this in the middle of a wood?" She turned and stared at him accusingly. "I can't believe I've been down here in deepest, darkest Dorset for two whole weeks, bored out of my mind, and only now do you think to show me this place." Joe looked deflated, and Maya thought she might have been a bit hard on him. She grinned and did a twirl, making the floorboards creak beneath her. "Better late than never, though, eh? It's wicked, Joe!"

Joe eyed the rickety staircase anxiously. "It looks dangerous to me."

"Come on!" she cried, and flew up the stairs, taking them three at a time. The ancient timbers groaned and shifted under her weight, but she was too excited to notice. She came to a crooked passageway with doors leading off it. She stopped, the smile fading from her face. Was that a door closing at the far end?

It was probably just the wind.

"Come on up, cuz!" she yelled at Joe.

He eventually arrived, having climbed the stairs much more carefully.

Maya led the way down the passage, deciding not to mention the closing door – she didn't want to scare Joe off just after finally tempting him in.

Opening a door on her left, she found a room piled high with very old cardboard boxes. Some of them were so full, or so squashed by those stacked above them, that they had split. Papers, yellow with age, were spilling onto the floor. Maya picked one up. It was a copy of a letter, dated 1st May 1956, addressed to someone in Dorsetshire County Council and signed Michael Doyle. He was asking if they had any information about his twin brother, a "missing evacuee" called Daniel Doyle.

Maya glanced up, her skin prickling. Was someone watching them?

No, it was just this house, giving her the creeps! She picked up another letter. It was addressed to the same official and was another enquiry from Michael Doyle about his missing brother, this time dated 1st June 1956.

"Michael Doyle, Daniel Doyle," muttered Joe, who was leafing through another pile of papers on the far side of the room. "Do you think they used to live here?"

Her curiosity now aroused, Maya picked up a whole sheaf of letters from the floor and began going through them. They were all virtually the same, except for the dates, which were always one month apart. She stared again at the papers scattered about her feet like autumn leaves, and then at the mountain of boxes piled up in front of her. "OMG!" she said. "This guy must have spent his whole life searching for his brother."

"What was that?" said Joe suddenly.

"I said this guy must have–"

"Shhh!" hissed Joe, glancing anxiously at the door. "I heard a noise outside."

"Probably a rat," said Maya, shivering slightly.

"Let's get out of here," said Joe.

But Maya wasn't ready to leave yet. These letters, the sheer number of them, in this abandoned old house – it was creepy, yet so intriguing!

Suddenly, they heard a thundering outside, as if someone in heavy boots was approaching. Maya and Joe went rigid with fright. There was nowhere to run. The boxes were blocking access to any window.

They both jumped as the door flew open. Staring down at them was an old man – a very old man – with bright blue eyes starting from his head. In his shaking hands was a shotgun, the muzzle pointing at Maya and Joe.

"What are you doing in here?" he demanded. "Get out of my house before I shoot the pair of you!"

Maya could see that the man was almost as scared as they were. And, by the way he was shaking, he was unlikely to hit either of them, except by accident. She swallowed and forced herself to be brave. "Hi," she said as calmly and cheerfully as she could manage. "I'm Maya. This is Joe. We're sorry if we've broken into your house. We didn't think anyone lived here."

The old man shouldered the weapon and took a more careful aim at Joe. "If you two snoopers aren't out of here by the time I count to five, I'll fire. I'm within my rights you know. I could shoot you both! He looked like he meant it. "One…!" he shouted. "Two…!"

Joe made for the door.

"Three…!" bellowed the man.

"Come on!" Joe shouted desperately at Maya. But she didn't move. There was something about this man. It wasn't just fear and rage she could see in his eyes, but a whole world of sadness. She knew then that he was Michael Doyle, the writer of all these letters. Maybe they could help him, if they could just….

"Four…!"

"Wait!" shouted Maya. "We can help you find your brother!"

The old man blinked and lowered his weapon. Then he took aim again. "What can a pair of kids like you do?"

Maya sensed Joe staring at her wide-eyed. She knew he was probably quietly freaking out, but she couldn't stop now. "We can find your brother, Mr Doyle," she said. "Trust us! We really can!"

The old man's anger flickered and died, and the creases around his eyes formed into lines of sadness. They seemed to be the natural contours of his face. The gun muzzle sagged towards the floor as his eyes roamed the mountain range of boxes in the room. "I've spent my whole life looking for him," he said. "I've written to every government department, every evacuee organization. I've put messages in the newspapers, on the Internet. It's like he never existed…." Michael Doyle's lips trembled with long-nurtured resentment.

"But he did exist! We were both evacuated here, as youngsters, in 1940."

He slowly sank down onto a box, lost in his memories. "We were glad to get away from London – Danny especially. He'd always had a sense of adventure that kid. Reckless some called him. I was quieter, more cautious…."

His voice trailed away as he choked back a tear.

"Go on, Mr Doyle," urged Maya gently.

The old man pulled himself together and continued.

"Our lives until then had been miserable. Dad was ill most of the time and couldn't get a job. We hardly had enough money for food – didn't even have a bed to sleep in. We'd never seen the countryside before we came to Dorset. A very happy year we had in Charlton Abbas. Well, apart from that business with Simon Kellaway…."

"Simon Kellaway?" exclaimed Joe. Charlton Abbas was his home village, and he knew the Kellaways. They were still a rough bunch.

"Yes, a big old bully he was, and he had it in for Danny. But apart from him, it was great – best time of our lives – that is until the night Danny disappeared."

Maya glanced at Joe, who was listening intently to the old man.

"I don't suppose either of you are twins," said Michael. "It's hard to explain. It's not like losing a brother – more like losing part of yourself. I've never been right since I lost Danny." He pulled a grubby handkerchief from his pocket and dabbed his eyes.

"I'm sorry," murmured Joe.

"I just wish I knew where he went to that night and why he never came back."

"Didn't the police try and find him?" Joe asked.

"For a bit," replied Michael. "But this was wartime, remember. They had more important things to worry about."

Maya was glad to see that Joe was as hooked as she was by Michael's story. She noticed Joe's hand had slid into the pocket where he kept his timephone – the device they could use to travel back into history. Joe must have been thinking the same thing she was. They hadn't used the phone since the previous summer when they'd gone back to 1840 to solve the mystery of Maddie Musgrove, the young maidservant hanged for stealing her mistress's jewellery. Maya hoped the phone still worked.

"When exactly did Danny disappear?" Joe asked.

"The 19th of April 1941," said Michael. "The date is engraved in my memory. The last time I saw him was that afternoon. He told me he was on his way to a warehouse near Beaminster. Danny had got himself a job with a local businessman, a dodgy fellow named Dawkins – I just thought it must be something to do with that. Then, at about half past six that evening, Mrs Morrison – she was the village postwoman – she was driving back from the sorting office in Bridport with some deliveries when she said she saw Danny running through Vipers' Fold, that very field out there."

The children turned and looked through the dirty window into the meadow beyond.

"Someone was chasing him, so she said, but she couldn't make out who. She told the police it looked like just a children's game and so she thought no more of it. As far as I know, she was the last person to see my brother."

Maya and Joe exchanged glances. They both knew what they wanted to do, but how do they explain it to Michael?

"Mr Doyle," said Maya, "we think we can help you."

"Do you have a photo of the two of you? I mean from the time you were evacuees?" Joe asked.

Michael rifled through one of the boxes and eventually handed Joe a tatty old photo. "Taken in 1941," he said, "just a few weeks before Danny disappeared."

The black and white image showed two curly-haired boys standing side by side in the front garden of a cottage. One was grinning cheekily, the other looking more serious. Apart from that, they were uncannily alike.

"Mind you, that was taken after a year eating decent country food. You should have seen us when we first arrived. Dirty street urchins we were, thin as sticks."

"Well, thank you, Mr Doyle," said Joe, handing the photo back. "I think we have all we need." He ushered Maya towards the door.

"Hang on a minute," said Michael. "What are you planning to–?"

"You'll see," said Joe with a grin.

If you would like to order this book, visit the ReadZone website: www.readzonebooks.com

FICTION EXPRESS

The Time Detectives:
The Disappearance of Danny Doyle
by Alex Woolf

When the Time Detectives, Joe and Maya, stumble upon
an old house in the middle of a wood, its occupant has
a sad and strange tale to tell. Michael was evacuated to
Dorset during World War II with his twin brother, Danny.
While there, Danny mysteriously disappeared and was
never heard from again. Can Joe and Maya succeed where
the police failed, journey back to 1941 and trace Michael's
missing brother?

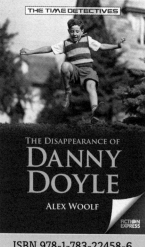

ISBN 978-1-783-22458-6

FICTION EXPRESS

The School for Supervillains
by Louie Stowell

Mandrake DeVille is heading to St Luthor's School for Supervillains, where a single act of kindness lands you in the detention pit, and only lying, cheating bullies get top marks. On paper, Mandrake's a model student: her parents are billionaire supervillains, and she has superpowers. The trouble is, Mandrake secretly wants to save the world, not destroy it.

ISBN 978-1-783-22460-9

FICTION EXPRESS

Drama Club
by Marie-Louise Jensen

A group of friends are involved in their local youth
drama club at a small city theatre. When their leader, the
charismatic Mr Beaven, announces he wants to put on
a major new play at the end of the summer holidays,
the cast is very excited.

Amidst rivalry, hopes and disappointments, will there
be more drama on or off the stage?

ISBN 978-1-783-22457-9

About the Author

Alex Woolf was born in London in 1964. He played drums in a teen band, and, in his 20s, he rode his motorbike and travelled in America (where he nearly ended up as a barracuda's lunch!). In between, he did lots of dull and dangerous jobs. His worst job was washing up in a restaurant kitchen full of cockroaches!

Finally, he settled down to write books. Alex has written non-fiction books on subjects like sharks, robots and the Black Death, but his greatest love is writing fiction, and he claims to have been writing stories almost since he was able to hold a pen.

His books for Fiction Express include *The Disappearance of Danny Doyle* (the second title in his Time Detectives series) and *Mind Swap*, a story in which a bully and his victim change places. He has also written *Chronosphere*, a science fiction trilogy about a world in which time moves super-slow, and *Aldo Moon and the Ghost of Gravewood Hall*, a story about a teenage Victorian detective who investigates ghosts in a spooky old mansion.